MARLEY AT THE ZOO

by Barnaby Stew

bb bebinsbooks.com

ISBN 978-1-950956-00-5 (paperback)

Walking at the zoo
with Momma and Daddo

and I just found an
animal shadow!

WHICH
Animal
IS IT?

IT'S AN...

Elephant!

Watching at the zoo
with Momma and Daddo

and I just found an
animal shadow!

WHICH
Animal
IS IT?

IT'S A...

Giraffe!

Sitting at the zoo
with Momma and Daddo

and I just found an
animal shadow!

WHICH
Animal
IS IT?

IT'S A...

Lion!

Spying at the zoo
with Momma and Daddo

and I just found an
animal shadow!

WHICH
Animal
IS IT?

IT'S A...

Monkey!

Riding at the zoo
with Momma and Daddo

and I just found an animal shadow!

WHICH Animal IS IT?

IT'S A...

Zebra!

**Standing at the zoo
with Momma and Daddo**

and I just found an
animal shadow!

WHICH
Animal
IS IT?

WAIT – THAT'S NOT
AN ANIMAL!

IT'S A
Car!

It's time to go home,
but we'll come back soon!
Bye-bye zoo!

BYE-BYE, MARLEY!

For more work by Barnaby Stew, visit
barnabystew.com/news

Made in the USA
San Bernardino, CA
23 May 2020

72195302R00020